the Shoe People™

CAN YOU KEEP A SECRET?

by James Driscoll
Illustrated by Rob Lee

Storm Publishing

D1313500

In a town not too far from here there is an old shoe repairer's shop. The outside of the shop looks very run down. There is a curtain across the window which looks quite dirty and torn. The window could really do with a good clean.

The front room of the shop is where the shoe mender keeps his tools so that he can mend shoes and boots which are damaged or worn out.

When he has repaired them they are put on shelves ready for their owners to collect. Some people are very forgetful and never come back to collect their shoes or boots.

Other people bring shoes and boots to him which are so badly worn that he cannot repair them. They ask the shoe mender to throw them away. BUT HE JUST CAN'T.

The shoe mender loves shoes and boots and even when they are worn out and of no further use, he still likes to keep them.

At the back of his shop there is a room which is very dusty and full of cobwebs. The floor is covered with boxes and tea chests. There are shelves around the walls and the shoe mender keeps all the shoes and boots that have been left behind in this room. He has put them in here for years and years and that is the reason it is piled high with so many.

This room has a very SPECIAL SECRET that only one person knows about. Who do you think that person could be?

No, not the old shoe mender. The only person who knows the secret is me.

CAN YOU KEEP A SECRET? CAN YOU? PROMISE?

Very well, if you promise, I will share the best kept secret in the world just with you.

The door which leads into the back room of the shop does not fit very well. Every night when the shoe mender goes home he has to pull it very hard so that it will shut. After he has slammed it shut, he goes out of the front door and locks up the shop.

He thinks that all is now quiet for the night, but just look what happens as the door slams . . .

A large cloud of dust fills the room and as the dust settles the STRANGEST THING takes place.

A worn out boot with a big hole in its toecap starts to move. Two eyes appear, then a nose and a mouth. He even has a tooth. He has yellow hair and wears a red hat. This is Trampy.

He looks all round the room and then puts his fingers to his mouth and whistles. This tells all the other shoes and boots that the time has come for more adventures and they all come to life.

On the top shelf there is P.C. Boot the policeman sitting next to Sergeant Major who has spent years and years in the Army. On top of the tea chest stands Charlie, the clown, with his yellow balloon and next to him a very pretty ballerina called Margot. There are many more Shoe People characters and you will meet them soon.

The room has now changed completely and we are in the Magic World of THE SHOE PEOPLE.

Welcome to Shoe Town. In this Magic World, shoes and boots become real just like you and me.

The Shoe People live in special houses.

The house which looks like a circus tent belongs to Charlie the clown. He is very funny and full of tricks. Charlie's house is called The Little Big Top.

The house with the crooked chimney and some of the paint peeling from the door belongs to Trampy. He's not very keen on house repairs or housework. He doesn't like gardening very much either. His garden is completely overgrown with wild flowers. Trampy's house is called Tumbledown House.

There is a red flag flying from the flagpole at the side of this house. Sergeant Major lives here. He always speaks in a very loud voice. In fact you might say he shouts. This is because he still thinks he is in the Army.

Sergeant Major's house is called Drill Hall. Sergeant Major has the best kept garden in Shoe Town. His lawn has the straightest stripes and the tidiest borders. Even the flowers stand to attention in this garden.

This pretty thatched cottage belongs to Margot, the ballerina. Her garden is full of beautiful sweet scented flowers of every colour of the rainbow. Margot waters her flowers every day and she says that is the reason they always look so beautiful.

Margot's house is called Swan Lake Cottage.

Wellington, being Wellington of course, doesn't like fine, sunny days. He much prefers rainy, stormy weather. Wellington has a very special play house in his garden so that even on fine sunny days he can do what he likes best — HE CAN GET VERY, VERY WET.

The house on the corner of Shoe Street with the big blue lamp hanging outside is where the friendliest policeman in the whole world lives. He is called P.C. Boot and he lives at Shoe Street Police Station, of course.

Now that you know the secret of the Magic World of The Shoe People — Remember! Only tell those of your friends YOU KNOW can keep a secret and be sure to make them...

PROMISE!